UNICORN PUBLI
P. O. Box SS 5574, Nassau
unicornmw@hotm
www.bahamasunic

SOMEBODY
Bahamas Short Stories
by Michael Wells
2019

Author & Publisher: Michael Wells
Editor: Lesley Spencer
Business Manager: Roderick Wells
Executive Assistants: Shirley E. Francis; Cheryl Wells;
Darius Williams
Business Services compliments of
Diane Phillips & Associates

Previously published
2017: Golden Heart

2015: Murder on the Eastern Road

2013: Fairweather Friends

2011: Change of Heart

2008: Love on Rose Island

2007: A Secret Life

2005: Africa Diamonds

The Unicorn magazine

From the Author

Michael Wells

It is with great joy that I announce that my eighth book of short stories has been published. God has instilled in each person on this planet a special gift. Some people have the gift of cooking, some the gift of sewing clothes, while others have the gift of telling stories or gardening.

One of the most talented people I know is Eric Minns, a musician, painter and writer. He has always been a great support to me and illustrated my first seven books. Now I'm sorry to say that that ill health has prevented him from illustrating this one. My very best wishes go to Eric Minns and his wife Laura.

I am truly grateful to my friend Candace Brown who took up the challenge to become the illustrator for this book.

Some people think they're not talented because they can't do certain things but because you can't write stories or illustrate doesn't mean that you don't have talent.

Twenty-five years ago, I didn't know I had the ability to make up stories and write. It was not until they attached a unicorn stick to my forehead that I started to write. I made many mistakes when I first started and it was very frustrating but I didn't give up.

Nobody knew my potential but, once I was given the right tools, I was able to be productive. If I had given up, the things that are occurring now would not be happening.

Everybody has to choose whether to be productive and make a difference in the world or just to sit and do nothing. I had no idea when I first started writing that it would lead to a Bahamian film producer, Mr. Kareem Mortimer, filming a documentary about my life.

With God's help, I developed my talent and now I am able to inspire people and with the money I earn from selling my books I can buy certain things that I want.

I encourage my loyal readers to develop their talents and see how far they will take you.

May God bless you.

Michael Wells.

Dedication to Monique Forbes

There have been many people over the years who have touched my life in a meaningful and tangible way. They have made my life richer and happier by their presence and by what they have done and continue to do.

One such person is Monique Forbes.

Monique attends St. Anne's Church which is located in Fox Hill and she is a nurse. Sometimes after church Monique would come down to see me, she would give me a bath and sometimes she would carry me to the carnival. Monique also carried me on my first cruise on board the Carnival's Legend. And one time I slept by her.

I am delighted to dedicate my eighth book of short stories to my dear friend Mrs. Monique Forbes.

Thanks, Monique, for all that you have done for me and for what you continue to do.

May God bless you.

Foreword

by Reverend Fr. Hugh A. Bartlett Jr.

Rector, Saint Anne's Anglican Church
Fox Hill & The Eastern Roads, N.P.

It is a great pleasure to be asked to provide this Foreword, and I wish to congratulate Michael on this work. Indeed, there are many among us who bury their abilities for fear of critics, or their own negative opinion of themselves.

I am personally proud of the stellar efforts of Michael, and his determination. He epitomizes one who sees the goodness of God in all things, which indicates a heart accepting of Providence. Yet we witness a will that is driven by ambition, self-worth, and independence.

"For even when we were with you, we gave you this command: Anyone unwilling to work should not eat. For we hear that some of you are living in idleness, mere busybodies, not doing any work."

2 Thessalonians 3: 10 -11

This is what I see in Michael, which is a man seeking to look after himself rather than settling for handouts. A man busy caring for himself rather than being a pest. There are so many clichés that may sound wonderful, but the genuine article is the work that Michael continues in his writings. Perhaps the name of Michael Wells will one day be used as a cliché to describe a man of determination.

Michael's efforts as a writer are an example to all and particularly to persons with physical challenges. There is a story in his book *"Love on Rose Island and Other Short Stories"* entitled *"It Cannot Happen to Me"*. In this story Michael highlights the need for all to be sensitized to the plight of people with challenges. Life can bring strange twists to any of us through accidents or illnesses, therefore, our views in life ought to be embracing of all people in any circumstance. The truth is that - "It Can Happen to Me."

Michael, I continue to offer my prayers and support, and to all readers of his work from his wonderful mind may we all be touched and inspired to use our abilities to make our world better.

Reverend Fr. Hugh A. Bartlett Jr.

Illustrations

by Candace Brown

Candace Brown has a Master's Degree in Business Management and is a florist, artist, illustrator and amateur actress. She has performed at the Bahamas Historical Society in a skit called 'Olden Days in Fox Hill' written by Mrs. Harolene Munnings-Brown, which can be viewed on YouTube.

Candace and Michael met in the summer of 2011. They became fast friends and she was soon hired to be his care giver. She carried out these duties until 2015.

Now, four years later, she has been asked to illustrate his books and since she has experience in this area, from illustrating the books from 'The Fox Hill Parade' series, she was quick to agree. Some of her work can be seen on her blog: **stronglife.wordpress.com**.

She feels it is a blessing from God to be able to add visuals to Michael's already graphic short stories and hopes they complement each other.

She congratulates Michael on his accomplishment of writing over 100 short stories and articles.

She thinks of him as 'One of God's **special** creations!'

Introduction to Michael

by Diane Phillips

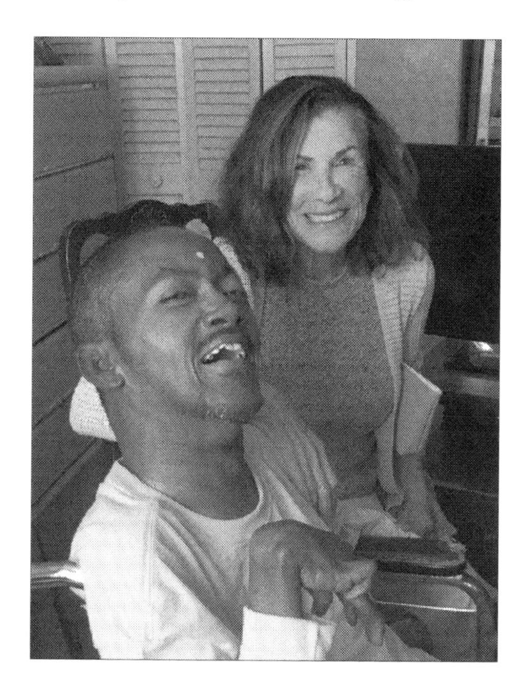

The Best of Michael Wells

It has been nearly 30 years since I first met Michael Wells and I have to confess he has aged better than I. In the decades since our first meeting when I recognized that the young man in his early 20s was bright beyond his ability to express it he has learned so much.

His desire to become a writer has blossomed into a career as one. His knowledge of the world around him has expanded faster than a waistline over the holidays. His spelling and sentence structure, thanks in large part to the ever-faithful editor-in-friendship Lesley Spencer, has scooted along a sliding scale from an F for performance if an A for effort to straight A's on both.

But some things about Michael have not changed and those are my favourite things. The way his eyes light up and say all the things his silence cannot when a friend enters the room. The way he does not pretend to hide his displeasure when he sees injustice or when something troubling infiltrates his space. Maybe it is because he cannot speak the way most of us can he has learned to slice through the fake politeness and cut to the chase with his eyes and the way his mouth turns.

See, the thing about knowing Michael is this. If at first you feel sorry for him thinking he is a great mind trapped in a dysfunctional body, if you think what a shame, here is a man who could have lived so rich a life if only he had been able to move his arms, legs, torso. If your heart aches because you wonder how bad it would be not to be able to scratch what itches or feed yourself or pull a shirt over your head, stop. Just stop right there.

Look at it Michael's way. That is one thing I have learned over the years, to stop feeling pity and instead feel pride. Michael Wells was given a brain and a heart, he was given life and a purpose, and he made the most of both.

His is not a story of a lesser among us. It is a story of courage, perseverance, fierce determination and success. It is a tale that can teach all of us a lesson about grabbing hold of what we have and running with it until we have used our last breath trying.

So now I join his many friends and followers in applauding Michael as we turn the pages of this, his eighth book of short stories.

Congratulations and love to you, Michael, even if you did age better than I.

Diane Phillips

Website

Michael has a website

www.bahamasunicorn.com

Which is run for him
by Dan Mullins

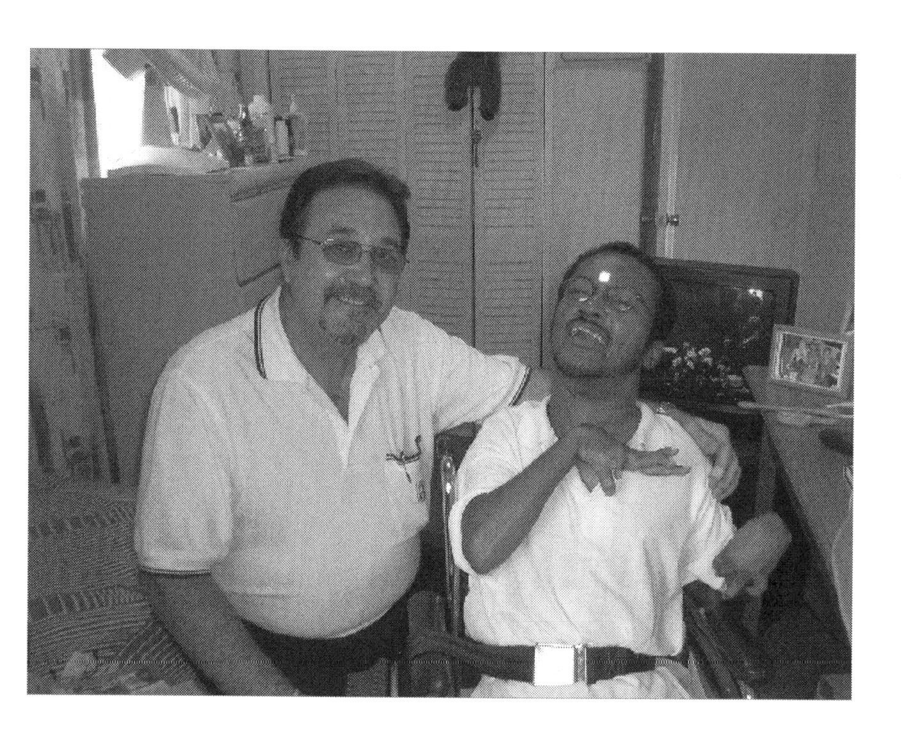

You can visit Michael's website
or email him at:

unicornmw@hotmail.com

TABLE OF CONTENTS

I CAN BE SOMEBODY

By Michael Wells.

Roberta walked out the front door of her luxurious house, jumped into her shiny Mercedes Benz and drove to Diamonds International. When she was about to enter the store, she saw her friend, a slender, fashionably dressed lady walking in the street.

'Hi Virginia,' she called out.

'Hello, Roberta. How are you?'

'I'm fine.'

Virginia waited till she caught up with her and then said confidentially: 'When was the last time you saw Maury?'

'That loser? I saw him the other day. He's so pathetic. Do you see the kind of clothes he wears?'

'Child, he can't do any better. He's so boring'.

'He must get those clothes from the dump,' said Roberta laughing.

'Some people just can't do any better. They can't be glamorous like us. Are you going to Janet's party on Friday night?'

'Yes, I am but I have to get a new outfit.'

'Me too. You know I have to look my best.'

'But you always do. Are you going into this store?' asked Roberta.

'Yes. I have to get a gift for my auntie.'

Roberta and Virginia walked into Diamonds International and Roberta purchased a beautiful diamond necklace. Virginia purchased a gold watch. As they left the store, they saw Maury by the roadside helping a lady change her car tyre.

'Look at that pathetic man. He can't do anything right?' said Roberta.

'Hi Maury. Why don't you get a life and stop being a nobody?' said Virginia.

'What happened? Couldn't you find anything on the dump?' added Roberta.

'Why don't you two leave me alone? Why are you always teasing me?' said Maury as he tightened the nut on the tyre.

'Let's leave the cry baby alone because he's just a nobody,' said Virginia.

'We tease you because we don't like you,' said Roberta.

'That's right. You should go somewhere and die because you'll never be anything. Just go and get lost,' added Virginia.

The old lady who Maury was helping spoke up: 'Why don't you young ladies leave this man alone. I don't know what's going on between you all but it seems to me you're being mean to him for absolutely no reason. Leave him alone.'

'You finally found a friend,' said Roberta. 'You two losers deserve each other. Let's go.'

Roberta and Virginia walked to their car.

'I have to get some shopping. I'll call you later.'

'OK darling.'

Roberta jumped into her car and drove home. She walked into her bedroom, slipped on her bikini bathing suit and walked outside through a beautiful garden to the pool. She was sitting in a lounge chair, enjoying the warm sun and sipping on a cocktail when her mother Catherine appeared beside her looking anxious and sad.

'I have bad news,' she said.

'What is it?' asked Roberta.

'Your father called and said that the company is in financial trouble. We have to sell our house and cars.'

'I don't understand. What does this mean?'

'It means we have to cut out the luxuries.'

'You mean no more parties and cruises?'

'That's right. And you'll have to get a job.'

'How do I do that?'

'We'll figure it out. In the meantime, we have to get a smaller house because it's too expensive to live here anymore. And we have to let the housekeeper go.'

'Are you serious?'

'I'm very serious.'

'Where will I find a job?'

'Look in the newspaper. Ask around.'

'I don't want my friends to know I'm poor. What would they say?'

'You can't worry about what your friends think. From now on you have to support yourself financially.'

'I'll look for a job and hope none of my friends see me.'

Roberta changed her clothes and drove to the Mall at Marathon so she would have time to think. She was walking around when she saw one of her friends.

'Hi Lakeisha. How are you?'

'I'm fine. I heard about what happened. I'm so sorry,' said Lakeisha.

'Thanks. We have to make a few changes to how we do things, but we'll make it. How did you find out about it so fast?'

'Social media. You know you can't keep a secret around here.'

'That's true.'

'What will you do?'

'I don't know. I have to help my parents.'

'It's good you're helping.'

'Do you know anyone who'd like to buy a car? I have to sell mine.'

'I'll ask around.'

'Thanks.'

As she walked along she saw Virginia. She hailed her but her former friend pretended she didn't know her and looked the other way. Roberta felt bad. She left the mall with her head hung low.

She picked up a newspaper and studied the jobs column. She made a decision, jumped in her car and drove across the island to a business in Sandyport. She asked the receptionist if she could see the person in charge and was shown into a large office.

'Maury! What are you doing here?' said Roberta in surprise.

'Ms. Bain, the lady whose tyre I was changing when you and Virginia were teasing me, owns this company. I'm in charge of human resources.'

'That's great for you,' replied Roberta looking at her feet.

'It's good working here. Ms. Bain is such a nice person.'

'I'm happy for you.'

'What brings you this way?'

'I need a job,' Roberta hardly dared speak the words, 'and I saw in the paper you're hiring.'

'We are. We need someone to work in the accounts department.'

'I know I've been mean to you and that I treated you badly. I hope you can forgive me and not hold the things I did against me.'

Maury sat there looking at Roberta. He wanted to throw her out of his office, but he didn't.

'I know you're a good organizer,' he mused, 'and if I hire you I believe you could be an asset to the company.' There was a silence while he thought about it.

'For those reasons I will hire you.'

Roberta had been ready to walk out of the office and she was overjoyed when Maury told her she had a job. She went to work in the accounts department and was soon promoted. She realised Maury was a true friend.

The End

I LOST MY BEST FRIEND

By Michael Wells.

Branvill was standing in front of John Bull on Bay Street when Grace walked up, looking depressed.

'Hi Grace. How's everything with you?' the slender man asked.

'Not great,' said Grace with her Haitian accent. 'I'm looking for a job.'

'I may have one for you. My housekeeper is going to Trinidad and I need someone to look after my son Arnold,' Branvill said. 'Arnold has arthrogryposis.'

'What's that?' asked Grace.

'Arthrogryposis is a disease that affects the joints,' Branvill explained.

'So, what would I have to do?'

'You'd have to care for Arnold and do everything for him.'

'I think I could do that.'

'Do you want the job?'

'Yes, I do.'

With Grace by his side, Branvill walked to his Camry and jumped in. They drove to a blue and white house located in Coral Harbour. When they reached, they entered the neatly kept house and walked into the bedroom where Arnold was sitting in front of his computer.

'Arnold, this is Grace. Grace, this is my son, Arnold,' Branvill said introducing them.

'Hello, it's a pleasure to meet you,' said Arnold.

'It is nice to meet you, too,' Grace responded smiling.

'Daddy, I'm going to a meeting this evening,' said Arnold.

'Is the bus coming for you?'

'Yes, at five o'clock.'

'OK. Grace, can you please get Arnold ready around four thirty?'

'Sure, I can,' said Grace.

'In the meantime, can you please clean the living room.'

Grace found cleaning materials and started working in in the living room. She was dusting the furniture when the doorbell rang and she went to answer it.

'Is Branvill home?' asked a dark-skinned lady.

'Yes, he is.'

'May I see him?'

The medium-sized woman walked into the living room where Branvill was reading the newspaper.

'Hi Jada,' said Branvill.

'I've come to find out if you still want to go to the show,' said Jada.

'Yes, we're still going,' said Branvill.

'Who's the woman who answered the front door?' asked Jada.

'Her name is Grace and I just hired her as a housekeeper.

'What's she supposed to be doing?' asked Jada in a hostile manner.

'What do you mean?'

'My friend hired a housekeeper and she came home one day and found her in bed with her husband.'

'You don't think I would do that?'

'I know one thing. If I even dream that anything is going on between you two, I will be your worst nightmare,' said Jada with fire in her eyes.

'Have I ever been unfaithful to you?'

'No and you better not start.'

'Grace is only here to clean the house and take care of Arnold, that's all.'

'I hope so.'

Just then Grace came back into the room.

'Excuse me. Would it be all right if I take Arnold for a walk?' she asked.

'Sure, you can. Whatever Arnold wants you can give it to him.'

'We'll just go a little way down the road.'

Grace walked into Arnold's bedroom and rolled him out the front door and down the road. As she did so, Jada stormed out to her Nissan and drove away.

'I don't think your father's friend likes me,' said Grace.

'What makes you think that?'

'I can tell by the way she looks at me.'

'Don't worry about her. She's a bitch and I don't like her either.'

'Does your father know how you feel?'

'He knows.'

'Well, I just met her and I don't like her,' agreed Grace.

'I don't know why Daddy got involved with her. He was seeing a nice lady but he dropped her when he met Jada.'

'Your Daddy made bad choice. One day he'll realize she's wrong for him.'

Grace pushed Arnold back home where they found Branvill sitting in the living room reading.

'Grace, I want to speak to you,' said Branvill. 'I'm going away to England and taking Arnold with me. Can you come with us to care for Arnold?'

'How long are you going for?'

'About three weeks. Can you come with us?'

'I've never been to England,' said Grace.

'Well, now you have an opportunity to travel there.'

'Thank you,' said Grace. 'I'd like to come.'

'It'll be a good trip and we'll have fun,' said Arnold.

'I'll make the travel arrangements and book the flights,' said Branvill.

He left the house and Grace rolled Arnold into the bedroom and changed him. There was a knock at the front door and she found Jada on the doorstep.

'Where's Branvill?' asked Jada.

'I don't know. He went out,' said Grace.

Jada walked through all the rooms of the house, looking at everything and searching. She went into Branvill's bedroom and looked inside all his drawers and closets. Then she went into the living room and searched through his papers on the coffee table. Without another word, she left the house and drove away.

'I wonder what she was looking for?' said Grace.

'I have no idea,' said Arnold.

'She's a strange woman.'

An hour after Jada left, Branvill returned.

'I booked the trip and we leave in two days' time.'

'That's great,' said Grace.

'I'm so excited about going to England,' said Arnold with a big smile.

'Your friend was here,' Grace told Branvill.

'I'll call her later. Take Arnold's suitcase out and start packing his clothes.'

Grace pulled down the suitcase from the bedroom closet and put Arnold's clothes inside. When she had finished, Branvill carried it into the living room.

'You need to get your clothes packed, too, Grace. I'll carry you home so you can pack.'

'I hope Jada doesn't think I'm trying to steal you from her because I'm not,' said Grace.

'Don't worry about her. I can handle her.'

'I hope so.'

Grace rolled Arnold outside and Branvill lifted him and sat him in the front seat while Grace hopped into the back. He folded the chair and placed it in the trunk and they drove to a house in the Grove.

Grace ran into the little wooden pink and white house. It didn't take her long to pack her suitcase and she carried it out and loaded it into the car.

When they arrived back at Branvill's, Jada was waiting in the driveway. She marched up to Branvill as he was helping Arnold out of the car.

'I hear you're going away!'

'Yes, I am. My son and I are going to England.'

'Will you be taking his nanny with you?'

'Yes. Grace is coming with us.'

'I see. I don't know what kind of game you're playing but you'd better be careful.'

'What are you so worked up about?'

'You're carrying this Haitian with you and you didn't ask me if I wanted to go?' said Jada angrily.

'I thought you were busy working.'

'You could still have asked but you chose to take this Haitian woman instead.' Jada glared at Grace hatefully.

'You don't have to carry on like this. There's absolutely nothing going on between me and Grace.'

'If you think you're going away with this woman, you're wrong. You watch what I'm going to do!'

Jada jumped into her car and sped off.

'What's her problem?' Grace asked.

'I don't know but I do know that I am tired of her suspicious mind,' said Branvill.

'She should trust you more.'

'I don't want to talk about Jada right now. Let's finish packing so that we can go.'

When they were ready, Branvill placed the suitcases by the front door.

'Before we leave tomorrow,' said Grace 'I want to see my friend. I'll be back in an hour.'

She left the house and Branvill went to see Arnold in his bedroom where he was watching The Youth Zone.

'This time tomorrow we'll be in England,' said Branvill.

'Can we ride on the big Ferris wheel in London?' asked Arnold.

'Sure, we can. And we'll also travel through the Channel Tunnel.'

'I know Grace would like that and so would I.'

Later that night they were eating their evening meal when the doorbell rang. A police officer was standing on the threshold.

'Are you Branvill Watson?'

'I am.'

'Do you know Grace Joseph?'

'Yes. Grace is my son's caregiver.'

'Grace's lifeless body was found in the bush on Cowpen Road with your contact information on her person.'

Branvill stood there in shock, hardly able to speak.

'How am I going to tell my son?' he finally said.

'Do you know anyone who would want to hurt Ms. Joseph?'

'No, I don't. She was a lovely woman. This is a real shock.'

'We would appreciate it if you could come to the morgue and identify the body.'

'I can't leave my son on his own. I'd have to bring him with me.'

'That will be fine.'

Branvill walked slowly into the bedroom and told Arnold what had happened. Arnold broke down and cried and his father put his arms around him to comfort him.

'She was my best friend,' said Arnold.

'We have to go to the morgue to identify her body,' whispered Branvill. Just as he said this the door opened and Jada appeared. Branvill told her what had happened.

'If you want to go, I'll stay here with Arnold,' she offered.

'Are you sure?'

'Yes,' I'm sure.'

Branvill made sure Arnold was OK, then he set out sadly for the morgue. As soon as he was gone, Jada came into Arnold's bedroom.

'Are you all right?' she asked.

'Yes, I am.'

'Would you like to sit in the living room for a while?'

'Thank you. I would.'

Jada rolled Arnold into the living room and switched on the television. A short time later there was a knock on the front door and Jada went to answer it. Arnold heard her exclaim in surprise and wheeled himself round so he could see the muscular man standing on the doorstep.

'Seth! What are you doing here?' asked Jada.

'The job is done. When do I get my money?'

'You'll get your money. Just give me a little time,' pleaded Jada.

'You have until tomorrow and remember the price is $80.000.'

'Don't worry! I'll pay you. I'm so happy that Haitian woman is dead. She was trying to take my man and I'll pay any amount to get rid of her.'

'I'll be waiting to hear from you.'

Arnold heard the whole conversation and he was appalled at what he heard. When Jada came back, he quickly pushed himself back in front of the television.

'Who was that?'

'Just a friend,' said Jada quickly, her cheeks flushed. 'I'm going to get something to drink. Would you like anything?'

'No, thank you,' said Arnold coldly.

He was happy to hear his father's car pull into the yard. When Branvill came into the living room Arnold told him what he had heard.

'Are you sure?'

'Completely. They were talking about having Grace killed,' said Arnold.

'We have to inform the police.'

Branvill pulled out his cell phone and dialled 919.

When Jada returned from the kitchen she acted as if nothing had happened.

'I didn't know you were back.'

'Yes, I just returned,' said Branvill.

'Were you able to identify Grace?' asked Jada.

'Yes. Sadly, it was Grace.'

There was a knock on the front door and two police officers came in.

'I'm Officer Jones and this is Officer McCoy. You called us?'

'I did. I just found out who murdered my housekeeper.'

'Really! Who is that?'

'That woman right there, Jada Ford.' Branvill pointed his finger at her.

'Who me? I didn't kill anyone,' said Jada.

'Yes, you did. Arnold heard you talking to your hired killer,' said Branvill. 'You took out a contract on Grace for $80,000.'

'You little piece of crippled garbage!' shouted Jada angrily.

The police officers struggled to put the handcuffs on her. Finally, they put her into the patrol car and drove to the police station where she spent the night. The police went searching for Seth and found him hiding out in Shady Tree Lane, Fox Hill. He and Jada appeared in court and were charged with the murder of Grace Joseph. Jada was also charged with hiring a hit-man. They were both sentenced to life in prison.

Arnold was glad to see the end of Jada. Branvill was more careful with his girlfriends after that. And he looked for someone else to take care of his son. Eventually, he found a young woman who was as kind and cheerful as Grace had been.

The End

I WANT TO ROLL WITH HIM

By Michael Wells.

Mariska was in the kitchen washing the dishes when there was a knock at the front door. She walked to the door and looked through the peephole.

'Who is it?' The short pretty lady asked.

'It's Janet.'

Mariska opened the door and tall lady stepped into the immaculately kept house.

'What's happening, girl?' Janet asked.

'Nothing much,' Mariska replied walking back into the kitchen.

'I just saw Daniel.'

'Oh yes?'

'He was going into Commonwealth Bank.'

'Daniel is trying to start his own business.'

'What type of business is that?'

'He wants to open a computer repair store on Prince Charles Drive. That's one thing I like about him. He's a very ambitious person and doesn't let the disability he has keep him back,' said Mariska with a smile that revealed the braces on her teeth.

'Why do I get the impression that you have a thing for Daniel?'

'And what if I do? He's a man and he has feelings, too.'

'Are you serious?'

'Yes, I'm very serious.'

'A pretty girl like you can have any man she wants.'

'I know that and I want Daniel.'

'That's your business but I know I wouldn't get involved with a half-dead man. It's OK being his friend but I can't see myself getting involved romantically with a man in a wheelchair,' said Janet.

'Why are you being so mean?'

'I'm going to find you a nice man because you don't seem to be able to find your own.'

'I don't know why you're so against him. Daniel is a nice, hardworking man.'

'I'm glad he's working but I still don't know why you want to be with him. I just don't understand it.'

'Well, you don't have to understand it,' said Mariska crossly.

'I'm going to find you a nice man who can walk,' Janet insisted with a determined look.

Mariska picked up her jacket. 'I'm going to see Daniel to find out if he needs help with anything.'

'Are you really serious about this?'

'Yes, I am.'

'You must be really hard up or else you're just being nice to him. I don't know which one it is but I hope you figure it out.'

'Don't worry about me, I know what I'm doing.'

'I hope so. I have to go and pick up my son. I'll see you later. Tell that cripple man hello from me.'

Janet walked out the door and Mariska went into her bedroom and freshened up. She jumped into her silver Honda and drove to a house in the Eastern Estates. When she arrived she walked up the ramp and rang the doorbell.

'Hi Daniel. How are you?' she asked smiling.

'I'm doing great. I just finished making cookies. Would you like some?' the well-groomed man asked.

'I would love some.'

With Mariska following him, Daniel rolled into the kitchen, opened the cupboard and pulled out a plate.

'You'll make some woman a good husband,' said Mariska.

'I don't know about that.' Daniel smiled as he put the cookies on the plate.

'Yes, you would.'

'I don't think any woman wants to marry me.'

'How do you know that? You just have to look around and you'll be surprised at what you find,' Mariska replied, her eyes sparkling.

'I have been looking around, and I haven't found anyone.'

'She's closer than you think,' said Mariska as she kissed him on the cheek.

'Really!'

'Yes.'

'I hesitate because I don't think any woman could handle my disability.'

'You don't have to worry about any woman because I love you and I want to be with you.' Mariska kissed him passionately.

'I have to think about this because I don't want to rush into anything.'

'You take your time, Sweetie, and I'll wait. But don't take too long.'

She hugged and kissed him again. 'I have to go to the store. Would you like me to get anything for you?'

'I can't think of anything right now.'

'Well, if you need anything just call me and I will get it and bring it for you. I've been invited to a party tonight. Would like to come with me?'

'Sure, I would.'

'Good. I'll pick you at 7:30 pm.'

Mariska walked out the door and Daniel sat there thinking about what she had said. Was she really serious? He logged into Skype and saw that his cousin Lawrence was on. He hailed him.

'What's happening, Lawrence?' Daniel asked.

'Nothing much. I was just checking my mail.'

'I just had a very interesting conversation with a pretty young lady.'

'Really? What was it about?'

'She wants to like me but I don't know if I should get involved with her.'

'Why not?'

'Because I'm afraid I might get hurt.'

'Who's the pretty lady you're talking about?'

'Mariska.'

'I know her. She is nice. Why do you think you'll get hurt if you get involved with her?'

'She might get tired of me and leave me.'

'In any relationship there's a possibility things may not work out. You just have to take the chance and pray that it works.'

'Do you think I should take that chance?'

'Only you can decide whether it's worth it or not.'

'I'll make that decision soon. Now I have to go and get ready because Mariska is coming for me.'

'OK, chat later.'

Daniel logged out of Skype and rolled into the bedroom to change. He sat on the porch and waited. An hour later Mariska pulled up.

'Wow! You look nice,' he said, manoeuvring out of his chair and into the car.

'Thank you,' replied Mariska as she folded the chair.

She placed it in the trunk, jumped into the driver's seat and drove to a house located in Winton. When they arrived, she removed the chair from the trunk and Daniel manoeuvred into it. With Mariska walking by his side, Daniel rolled through a beautiful garden and into the back yard where tables and chairs were set up.

'Would you like anything to drink?' asked Mariska.

'Yes, please. I'd like a rum and coke,' said Daniel.

Mariska went over to the bar and brought back the drink. She gave it to Daniel who took it and sipped.

Mariska and Daniel were enjoying themselves when Janet walked in with a handsome man.

'This is John, John this is Mariska,' she said.

'It's nice to meet you,' said John.

'John works as a manager at Atlantis and he also owns a restaurant. He's single too,' said Janet winking at Mariska.

'That's nice,' said Mariska.

'John is trying to improve his restaurant business. Maybe you can help him?' said Janet with a sly look.

'I don't know what I can do, but I'm willing to help,' said Mariska.

'You two can get together and get to know each other better and, who knows, maybe something will click between you,' said Janet with a wicked smile.

'What are you trying to do?' Mariska asked.

'Nothing. I'm just introducing you to this nice man who can walk,' said Janet.

'No! You are trying to get John and me together. But I see what you're doing and it won't work. You're my friend and you should respect my wishes,' said Mariska angrily.

Mariska and Daniel left the party and drove to Arawak Cay where they sat in the car and talked.

'I was thinking about what you said and I would just love to have you as my wife,' said Daniel.

'Really! I don't want you to do anything you don't want to do.'

'I am sure,' said Daniel with a smile.

Mariska kissed Daniel passionately. They were married that June and had two children. Daniel opened his computer repair shop and the business was a success.

Janet got married to a good-looking man but she quickly left her husband because he abused her physically and verbally.

The End

I REMEMBER YOU

By Michael Wells.

Harris was driving down John F. Kennedy Drive on his way to the airport to pick up a friend when a big dump truck came speeding along in the opposite direction. The driver lost control of his vehicle and hit a car. The truck jumped the median and slammed into Harris's car, totally demolishing it.

The ambulance and fire services arrived and they had to work frantically to cut him out of the mangled car. He was unconscious when they put him in the ambulance and rushed him to Princess Margaret Hospital. He underwent emergency surgery and was placed in an intensive care unit. When he regained consciousness, he had no idea what had happened or where he was.

As he studied the ward around him, a nurse came in.

'I'm going to be looking after you,' she said. 'My name's Nurse Dawson.

'What happened to me?' he asked.

The nurse told him about the accident.

'I can't remember anything about it.'

'Dr. Parker is coming to see you,' she said. 'You can ask him about it.'

When the doctor came, he examined Harris and spoke gently to him.

'Do you remember your name?'

Harris thought hard but then had to say: 'No.'

He asked him several other questions but Harris could remember nothing.

'I'm afraid you have amnesia.'

Harris was confused. 'When will I regain my memory?'

'I don't know. It could come back gradually or all at once. Anything could cause your memory to come back. It may come back soon, or it may take a while.'

When the doctor left, Harris lay in bed feeling all alone in the world. The days passed and no one came to visit him.

One day he was lying there trying to remember things when Nurse Dawson walked in. She changed the bed linen and put fresh water in the jug.

'So how is my patient doing today?' she asked, determined to cheer him up.

'I'm OK. I'm trying to remember my name. I think it might be Harris.'

'That's a great start. Well done. I will call you Harris.'

She laid out some magazines for him to read.

'And can you remember your surname?'

Harris shook his head.

'It's just so frustrating trying to remember and I can't.'

'Give it time. Your memory will return. Have you had any visitors?'

'No. It's like nobody knows I'm here.'

'I'm sure someone will come soon.'

The next morning Dr Parker came into the room and checked on him: 'How you doing today?'

'Besides not being able to remember anything before the accident, I'm fine.'

The doctor examined him and said: 'Physically, you've recovered. In my opinion, you can be released in a couple of days' time.'

'That's good, I'm tired of being in hospital.'

'Do you have anywhere to stay when you are discharged?'

'No. I don't know my name or my address. I suppose I must have a home somewhere.'

Harris began to think about where he would go when he left hospital. He was feeling depressed about it until one morning Nurse Dawson brought him a cup of coffee.

'If you like, you can stay with me when you are discharged,' she said. 'I have a spare room.'

'That's very nice of you to offer,' Harris said in surprise. But I can't intrude on you like that.'

'You wouldn't be intruding. I have a four-bedroom house, so there's plenty of room.'

'Won't your husband mind you bringing home a strange man?'

'I'm divorced and only my twelve-year-old daughter Marianne and I live there.'

'It's a very generous offer. Please let me think about it.'

'You think about it and let me know what you decide.'

By next day he knew what he wanted to do and he accepted Nurse Dawson's offer.

'Right,' she said. When you're discharged you'll come home with me.'

'I hope I won't be too much trouble,' said Harris sadly.

'You won't be any trouble. Your memory may soon return and you'll be able to go about your normal life.'

'I don't mean to be nosey but I'm curious. How come you're divorced?'

'My ex-husband, Florek, got involved with some very dangerous people and I didn't want to be a part of that kind of life. So, I divorced him.'

'I've only known you a few weeks but already I can see you're a really nice person. If I had to choose between you and some dangerous people, I would choose you.'

'Thanks for the compliment! Unfortunately, my ex-husband didn't feel the same way.'

'That's sad and he's the loser.'

When the time came to leave, Dr. Parker shook his hand. 'I'll leave you in Nurse Dawson's capable hands.'

Nurse Dawson helped Harris get ready to leave. They left the hospital, jumped into her Camry and drove to a pretty white and red house located in South Beach.

A young girl greeted them at the front door.

'Marianne, this is my friend, Harris. Harris this is my daughter, Marianne,' said Nurse Dawson introducing them.

'It is nice to meet you, Marianne,' said Harris.

'Nice to meet you, too,' said Marianne.

'Marianne, do you have any homework?' asked Nurse Dawson.

'Yes, I do.'

'Then go and finish it.'

'OK, Mommy.'

Marianne walked into her bedroom and settled down with her homework.

'You have a fine daughter,' said Harris.

'She is my heart string.'

'I don't understand how any man can give all this up.'

'Florek did. He doesn't even call to ask about Marianne or anything.'

'That's sad, but as I said, it's his loss.'

'Did you hear that?' asked Nurse Dawson suddenly.

'Hear what?'

'I heard a noise outside.'

Harris looked out the window and saw a tall, muscular man trying to break into the house. He chased the intruder away and called the police. The police looked around but could find no trace of the man.

When they left, Nurse Dawson and Harris sat in the front room and talked.

'I'm grateful to you for chasing away the intruder,' said Nurse Dawson.

'I'm grateful to you for giving me a home,' said Harris. As he spoke, he suddenly got a strange look on his face.

'What's wrong?'

'I'm remembering something. I see myself talking to a man about taking out a contract. But I don't know what the contract is about . . .'

'Maybe you're a builder and the contract is about building a house or an office?' Nurse Dawson urged him on to remember.

'I don't know. It's so frustrating.'

'Just give it time.'

'I just had another memory flash.'

'Tell me what you're remembering.'

'I'm discussing payment for a job with a man I'm supposed to work with.'

'What is the job?'

Harris struggled for a while. 'No. I don't remember.'

'You're doing well. Your memory is starting to come back.'

'I wish I could remember what type of job it was.'

'Don't try so hard. Relax and it will come.'

'I just want my life back.'

'You've been indoors all day, Let's go for a drive. Come on, the fresh air will do you good.'

Nurse Dawson called to Marianne and all three went outside and jumped into the car.

They were driving up Bay Street when they had to stop at a red traffic light. A yellow car pulled up next to them. Harris noticed there were two men in it but when he looked again he saw that one of the men had a gun and was pointing it straight at their car.

'Watch out!' shouted Harris. He leaned over and put his foot hard on the accelerator. The man with the gun fired just as Nurse Dawson's car leapt forward. The car hit a light pole and spun round while the other car sped off.

Harris cracked his head on the dashboard as the car collided with the pole. With difficulty he managed to struggle out of the car, holding his head, and go around to check that Nurse Dawson and Marianne were all right. They were shaken but not badly injured.

Police and ambulance arrived and the three of them were carried to the hospital.

The knock on the head caused Harris to regain his memory. At the hospital, as he sat in the waiting area, he sank his head into his hands. His whole life came flooding back to him and he was not proud of it.

'What have you remembered?' asked Nurse Dawson.

'You must forgive me,' he said. 'Please forgive me.'

'What do you mean?'

Haltingly, he told her that he was a hit man who had been hired by her ex-husband, Florek, to kill her and her daughter because he did not want to pay child support. He'd been on his way to carry out the contract when he was hit by the dump truck.

‘How could you!’

‘I’m so very sorry. Now that I’ve met you I see how wrong I was. I hope you can forgive me.’

Nurse Dawson was so shocked she walked out of the room.

Then she informed the police and they arrested both Harris and Florek. When the police questioned Florek he confessed that since the first hit man he hired had failed, he’d hired another one who tried to shoot them at the traffic lights.

Florek, Harris and the other men who were involved all appeared in court and were charged with a range of offences including attempted murder. They were sentenced to a total of twenty-five years in jail.

The End

MY FRIEND EATS TOO MUCH

By Michael Wells.

A white Odyssey pulled into Government High School yard and a plump lady jumped out. She walked to the back of the car, opened the trunk, removed the wheelchair and pushed it round to the passenger side.

'Come on Caroline,' Tara said to her daughter.

'OK, Mommy,' said Caroline as she maneuvered out of the car and into her wheelchair.

'Are ready for your first day at school?'

'I'm looking forward to it.'

Caroline rolled herself into the classroom, with Tara walking by her side. She felt nervous about meeting the other students.

'Class, we have a new student with us this morning, Ms. Caroline Miller. Let's welcome her,' said the teacher.

The whole class welcomed Caroline. She rolled to her assigned desk and settled down to work. When class was over, she rolled outside and was sitting under a dilly tree enjoying her snack when a girl walked up to her.

'Hi, my name is Mary. Can I sit next to you?' the pencil-sized girl asked.

'Sure you can.'

Mary sat down and opened a bag. She removed an apple, took a bite and put it back in the bag.

'Is that all you're eating?' asked Caroline.

'Yes, I don't want to get fat,' said Mary.

'Fat! You don't have an ounce of fat on you!'

'My father wants me to be a model and he says that models are not fat. So I have to watch my weight.'

'That's good but I would say you're too thin.'

'How else can I be a model? My father says there are no fat models.'

Caroline thought about this as she finished the tasty snack her mother had given her.

'Do you really want to be a model?'

'My father said models travel all over the world and make lots of money.'

'But is that what you want?'

'I guess.'

'You seem to be a nice girl and you're very intelligent. You shouldn't be forced into doing something you don't want to do.'

'You don't know my father. Everything has to be his way or the highway.'

'That sounds harsh.'

'That's the way he is.'

'What does your Mommy say about it?'

'She just goes with whatever Daddy says.'

'Do you think you would like to come by my house sometimes?' said Caroline.

'I'll ask but it should be OK.'

'Good. I'll ask my Mommy.'

Mary stood up 'I have to use the rest room. I'll be right back. 'She walked into the rest room and came back a few minutes later.

'What did you do in there?' asked Caroline suspiciously.

'Nothing. Just used the rest room.'

'You did more than that. I heard you.'

'Don't worry about it. I'll be alright.'

'Were you throwing up?'

'I have an upset stomach, that's all.'

'I'm concerned about you,' said Caroline.

'I'll be all right,' Mary repeated.

'Are you on Facebook? Can I add you?'

'Sure you can.'

Tara arrived and Caroline maneuvered out of her chair and into the car.

'I'll see you tomorrow,' she waved to Mary.

Tara put the chair in the trunk and jumped into the driver's seat.

'How was your day?' she asked.

'My day was interesting,' said Caroline and she told her mother about her new friend.

'Mary sounds like she needs help. Do you know if she gets counselling?'

'I don't think so.'

'It sounds as though she has a problem. I'm proud of you for wanting to help her.'

Tara pulled into the drive way and a tall man came outside and removed the wheelchair from the trunk. He pushed it to the passenger side of the car.

'Hi Daddy,' Caroline said as the man helped her out of the car and into the chair.

'How is Daddy's girl doing today?'

'I'm fine.'

'Did you have a good day at school?'

'Yes, I did.

'Ian,' said Tara to her husband, 'Caroline says she needs some help with her school project this evening. Can you help her?'

'And then I need to get some things from the store,' added Caroline.

'OK. After dinner we can do all that,' said Ian.

Later that day Caroline and her father went outside to his truck.

'I have to stop by Mr. Bain to pick up the lawnmower,' said Ian as he lifted her out of the chair and gently put her into the truck.

Ian folded the chair and place it in the back of the truck. He jumped into the driver's seat and drove to a house located in Deals Heights. When he rang the front doorbell, a short man opened the door.

'Hi, Darold. How's everything?'

'Everything is good,' replied Darold.

'That's great. I've come to get the lawnmower.'

'I have the lawnmower in my work shop.'

Darold opened the door of his workshop. While Darold was in his workshop Caroline saw his wife come out of the house. She could hear her clearly from the car.

'Did you tell Mary she can have a chicken sandwich?' the tall lady asked.

'No, Page, I did not,' said Darold.

'Well she's eating all kinds of things.'

'I'll talk to her.'

Page sent Mary to see her father in the workshop.

'Daddy, can I please have some ice cream?'

'No, Mary,' said Darold firmly.

'I just want a little bit.'

'I said no. Don't you see how much weight you've put on? That's because you don't listen to me and you eat too much. Now go inside. I'm busy.' Darold spoke harshly to his daughter.

'Do what your father says,' added Page.

Mary started to walk towards the house but her knees crumpled and she fainted. Darold, Page and Ian rushed over to her and tried to revive her. When they could not wake her up, they put her in Darold's car and rushed to the hospital.

At the hospital the doctor diagnosed her as anorexic. He told Page and Darold that Mary was underweight and malnourished. They had to give her plenty of food and make sure she gained weight.

Mary stayed in hospital and was fed intravenously. Caroline visited her and was sad to see her friend in such a sorry state. She wished she could do something to help her. Each day she brought her tasty snacks and fruit and sat by her bed, talked and prayed with her. Mary and her parents both received counselling and the situation improved. She started eating and gained weight.

Caroline was happy to see her friend making progress. She encouraged her to defeat her eating disorder. Page and Darold realised they were treating their daughter badly and starving her. They wanted her to be healthy and happy and gave up thoughts of her becoming a model.

The End

SECOND FIDDLE

By Michael Wells.

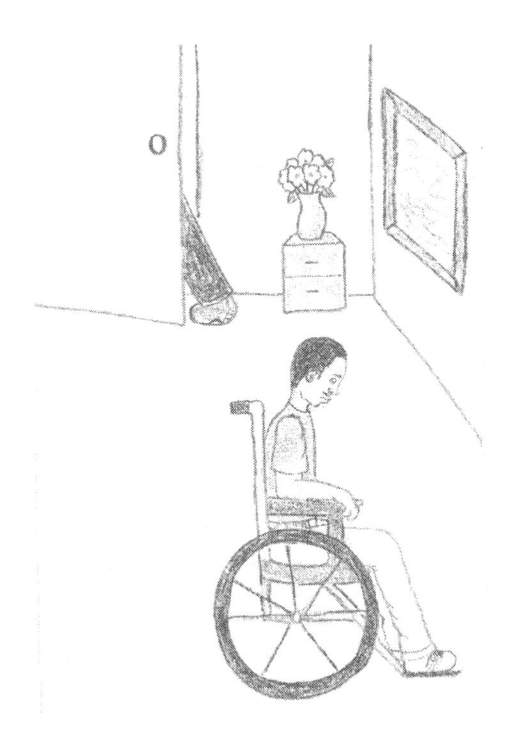

Denise was sitting on the porch enjoying the cool summer breeze when her neighbour, an old gentleman with white hair, walked onto the porch and greeted her.

'Hi, Denise. What's going on?'

'Hi, Nigel. Nothing much,' said the pretty young lady. 'But I need a job.'

'I thought you had a job.'

'I was working but the company closed down last month and I've not had a job since. I have two children to take care of, bills and rent to pay and I don't have any money.'

'Maybe I can help,' said Nigel. 'I need some cleaning done. If you are willing to clean, I will pay you.'

'That sounds OK. I can clean.'

'Good! Let's go.'

Denise walked next door with Nigel and entered his messy house.

'When was the last time you cleaned?' she asked, looking at the pile of clothes on the sofa.

'I had a lady come to work a few weeks ago but she didn't work out, so I let her go.'

Denise walked into the bedroom where Nigel's son was sitting in front of his computer.

'Hi, Bruce,' she said.

'Hi, honey. Have you come to keep me company?'

'Not really. I've come to work.'

'Instead of work, why don't we have a little party?' suggested Bruce with a mischievous look.

'You'd better behave!' Although she sounded cross, Denise couldn't stop a smile appearing on her face.

'I can't behave when I'm around you. How's your boyfriend, Brad?'

Denise rolled her eyes. 'I kicked him to the curve because he wasn't treating me right.'

'I see. So, do I have you all to myself?'

'I suppose you do.'

Bruce needed no more encouragement. He had not been able to stop thinking about Denise since she'd taken up with Brad.

'I really love you and I don't like sharing you. I don't want to be second fiddle.'

Denise sat beside him and took his hand. 'You don't have to worry about that.'

'That's good to know. How about you and me going out tonight?'

'I would like that. Where do you want to go?'

'How about the Fish Fry?'

'That sounds good. But how will we get there?'

'I'll ask my cousin Nick to carry us.'

'Sure.'

'So, we have a date?'

'Yes, we do.'

Bruce smiled, then he added with a sly look: 'And afterwards, maybe we can go to a hotel and chill out?'

'You are one hot man.'

'I'm hot for you baby.'

'You'd better cool down.'

'How are your children, Louis and Rachelle?'

'They're fine.'

When Denise went into the living room to begin cleaning, Bruce logged into Skype and found Nick was online.

'What's going on?' asked Nick.

'I need you to please do me a favour.'

'Sure, what is it?'

'I want to take my friend out to dinner and I need a chauffeur.'

'I would be delighted to assist you. What time do you want me to pick you up?'

'How about seven o'clock?'

'I'll be there,' said Nick.

Denise came back into Bruce's room.

'I just finished talking to Nick and everything's set,' he told her. 'He's coming at seven.'

'Great!' Denise replied.

That evening, Denise came back to the house, changed Bruce's clothes and rolled him outside in his wheelchair. A grey car pulled up and a well-groomed man with salt and pepper hair jumped out.

'Hi Bruce. Are you ready?'

'Yes, we are.'

'Is this beautiful lady coming with us?'

'Yes, she is,' replied Bruce with a big smile.

Nick lifted Bruce out of the chair and placed him in the car while Denise sat in the back seat. Nick put the chair in the trunk and drove them both to the Fish Fry.

When they arrived, Nick sat Bruce in his chair and snapped a photo of him with Denise beside him. Then he left them to enjoy their evening. Denise rolled Bruce down to Oh Andros and found them a seat.

'How about daiquiris and conch fritters to start with?' suggested Bruce.

'Sure,' said Denise.

The waitress brought their drinks and gave them menus. They looked them over and decided what they wanted. When the meal arrived, Denise used Bruce's fork to feed him.

'You make me feel good and I wish we could always be together,' said Bruce.

'I'm here to please you and do whatever you want me to do,' said Denise.

'I don't mean I want you to be my caregiver, I want you to be my girlfriend.'

'Let me think about it. '

'I really love you. '

'I believe you.'

'You mean the world to me and I would just love you to be my girlfriend,' Bruce insisted.

'I know you would but let me think about it.'

'OK, but I won't give up until I make you mine.'

'Really!'

'I'm determined to do all I can to achieve my goal.'

The rest of the meal passed pleasantly and they enjoyed the atmosphere of the busy Fish Fry.

'What else do you want to do?' asked Bruce when he had paid the bill.

'I don't know. What else do you want to do besides the obvious?' asked Denise.

'We could walk up to the beach.'

'Let's do that.'

Denise rolled Bruce towards the beach and parked his wheelchair beside a bench.

'Can I come and spend the day with you tomorrow?' he asked.

'Sure you can.'

'Good.'

Nick pulled up and put Bruce in the car. He folded the chair and placed it in the trunk while Denise got into the back seat. Nick hopped into the driver's seat and on the way home they stopped on Montagu Beach and took some more photos.

When they arrived at Bruce's house, Denise rolled him inside and parked him in front of his computer. Then she went back to her house.

Bruce logged into Skype and found Nick online. He hailed him.

'Thanks for your help this evening.'

'No problem. Any time,' said Nick.

Bruce poured out his heart to Nick. 'I really love Denise and I hope that she feels the same.'

'I hope so, too,' said Nick warmly. They spoke for a while, then Nick had to go and answer the doorbell. 'I'll talk to you later,' he promised.

Next day Denise invited Bruce over to her house. She rolled him into her bedroom and inserted a disc into the DVD player. She left him there watching TV. But a few minutes later she hurried back with a look on her face that told Bruce something was wrong.

'Would you mind moving into Grammy's room?' she said urgently. Before he could answer, she turned off the TV and started to move his wheelchair.

'Why?' asked Bruce.

'My friend Danny's come to visit me and we want to eat lunch,' said Denise.

'Why can't you eat lunch on the porch? '

'It'll only be a few minutes.'

'I've come over here to spend time with you and you're kicking me out because another man has come to you!' said Bruce angrily.

'I'll bring you back when he leaves.'

Denise rolled Bruce into her grandmother's bedroom and when she left he sat there with anger swelling up inside him. He couldn't believe Denise would treat him that way and he was hurt.

He planned to tell Denise how much she had hurt him. Three hours later she returned and Bruce gave her a hateful look.

'Do you think what you did was fair to me?' he asked.

'I don't know.'

'You underestimate my feelings for you. I told you I really love you and when I come over I come to be with you.'

Denise could not meet his eye. 'He helps me.'

'And is that supposed to justify you kicking me out of your room?'

'No, but I did bring you back after.'

'How would you feel if the person you love was seeing someone else? Would you be happy about it and pretend it was nothing? Or would you let the person know how you feel? '

'I would tell them how I feel.'

'I know I have limitations because of the physical disability I have and I may not be able to do certain things, but I have feelings just like everybody else. It hurts me to know you have someone else and it's not fair to expect me to sit around as though nothing is happening. I'm not going to pretend it doesn't upset me.'

'I'm sorry I hurt you. '

'You wouldn't like it if you were in my position and it's not fair to expect me to say nothing. I don't know of any sane person who would keep quiet. Besides,' he added, 'I don't just think of you as a caregiver but as my girlfriend and I really love you.'

Denise realized just how serious Bruce was and she stop seeing Danny. Although it was a little rough sometimes because of Bruce's physical disability, Denise stuck with him and they worked things out together. They were able to open a snack food shop and make some money.

Bruce was a good husband and stepfather to Denise's two children. Denise had another baby and they named him Bruce Junior.

The End

WHO WILL CARE FOR MY SON?

By Michael Wells.

Douglas jumped out of bed and went to the bathroom. When he was through, he walked into his son's bedroom.

'Good morning, Jake. Are you ready to get up?' The salt-and-pepper headed man asked.

'Yes Daddy, I am,' replied the handsome young man.

Douglas lifted Jake out of bed and sat him in his wheelchair. Then he rolled him into the bathroom, brushed his teeth and washed his face.

'What would you like for breakfast?' asked Douglas.

'I would like waffles, please.'

'Waffles it will be.' Douglas took the waffles out of the fridge and popped them into the toaster, then added: 'I don't feel too good today.'

'What's wrong?' asked Jake.

'I don't know. I just don't feel right.'

'Maybe you should go to the doctor?' suggested Jake. 'Or you could go next door and ask Nurse Rahming to check you out.'

'I'll be OK,' said Douglas, pushing the plunger down. 'What do you want to drink?'

'Apple juice, please.'

Douglas opened the fridge and pulled the apple juice.

'I have to take you to the barber today.'

'I still think you should go to the doctor,' Jake insisted.

'No, I'll feel better soon.'

When Douglas had finished feeding Jake, he put the plate in the sink and pushed him outside.

'Hi, Jake,' called a neighbour.

'Hi, Lisa.'

'Do you want to come over later? Mommy is cooking fish.'

'Oh yes! You know how much I like fish.' Jake gave her a big smile.

'When you come back, I'll come over and get you.'

'Lisa, where's your twin?' asked Jake.

'Latoya went to the store. She'll be back soon.'

'Remind Latoya she promised to cut my finger nails.'

'OK. I will.'

'Where is your one-inch tall niece?' asked Jake.

'Tina's inside,' said Lisa.

Just then a short, plump young lady waked out of the house.

'Hi, Tina,' called Jake.

'I'm going to on beach later. Would you like to come with me?' said Tina.

'Great. I'd like that.'

'When I come back from the store, I'll take you.'

Douglas lifted Jake out of his chair and put him in the front seat of his green Ford truck. He folded the chair and place it in the back of the truck. They drove to the barber where Douglas lifted Jake out and put him back in his chair.

While Jake was having his hair cut, Douglas picked up a magazine and was leafing through it when a tall man came into the shop.

'Hello everybody,' said the newcomer.

'Hello Frank! I haven't seen you since I left J.S. Johnson. How are you doing?' said Douglas as he stood up to shake Frank's hand.

'I'm doing fine. I just came back from Cat Island.'

'How are things up there?'

'Very good. How is your wife?'

'I'm afraid Mary died last year,' said Douglas.

'I'm sorry to hear that.'

'She was killed in a traffic accident.'

'That's terrible,' said Frank. 'You have my deepest sympathy.'

'She was a lovely lady.'

'I see you still have your son with you.'

'Yes, Jake and I are still together.'

'You're a good father and the Lord will bless you. Most men would just put him in Sandilands and wouldn't check for him.'

'I can't put my beloved son in Sandilands.'

'Do your brothers and sisters help with him?'

'Both my brother and my sister are dead,' said Douglas sadly, as he watched the barber cut Jake's hair.

'Well, it's good that you can take care of him.'

'I try my best.'

'That's all you can do.'

When the barber had finished cutting Jake's hair, Douglas paid him, then they left.

'See you later Frank.'

Douglas drove home via Super Value Food store. He left Jake in the truck, listening to the radio, grabbed a trolley and pushed it through the aisles collecting the items he needed. He loaded the back of the truck with the groceries and drove home.

He was about to carry his bags to the front door when Latoya appeared.

'Would you like me to help you?'

'I sure would. Thank you,' replied Douglas with a smile.

Latoya took some bags from the back of the truck and carried them inside. She began to unpack while Douglas lifted Jake into his chair and pushed him into the house.

'Jake, would you like to come over and watch a DVD with me?' asked Latoya removing the eggs from their bag and placing them in the fridge.

'Sure. What's the DVD?'

'Pirates of the Caribbean 2: Dead Man's Chest.'

'I should like that,' said Jake beaming with delight.

'OK, when I've put these things away, we'll go.'

'Has your Mommy started cooking the fish?' asked Jake.

'She just put it in the pan.'

Latoya finished putting away the groceries and then she pushed Jake next door to her house. A delicious smell wafted from the kitchen where her mother was in the kitchen frying the fish. Latoya pushed Jake into the living room and took the finger nail clipper to cut his nails.

Latoya's Mommy came in.

'Hi Jake,' said Mablean.

'Hello Ms. Rahming.'

Latoya spread Jake's fingers so he could see his nails had been cut. She put a DVD into the machine and picked up the remote control.

'You finished cooking?' Latoya asked.

'Yes, the food is ready,' said Mablean.

Latoya went into the kitchen, dished up some food and carried it into the living room to feed Jake. Lisa arrived and sat down to watch Pirates of the Caribbean 2 with them.

Later that night, Lisa pushed Jake home. When she rang the doorbell, Douglas slowly opened it, holding onto the wall. He did not look too well.

'What's wrong, Mr. Murray?' said Lisa.

'I have a severe headache and I feel like I'm going to vomit.' Douglas clutched his head and his stomach.

'Would you like Mommy to carry you to the hospital?'

'Yes, please.' Douglas went towards Jake's wheelchair and sank to the ground.

Lisa ran home and burst through the door.

'Mr. Murray doesn't feel well and he wants you to take him to the hospital,' she shouted to Mablean.

Mablean grabbed her car keys and rushed next door where Jake was looking at his father sitting on the stoop. Mablean and Lisa lifted Douglas and put him in the car.

'You stay with Jake while I take Douglas to the hospital,' said Mablean.

She drove away and Lisa pushed Jake back to her house. He was very worried about his father.

'Do you think Daddy will be all right?'

'Let's hope so. Try not to worry,' said Lisa.

'When do you think they'll be back?'

'I don't know.'

Tina came in and Lisa told her what had happened.

'How long have they been gone?' asked Tina.

'Quite a while.' said Lisa.

They switched on the DVD and tried to watch a film to pass the time.

Mablean came back very late that night.

'How's is my Daddy?' asked Jake fearfully.

'I'm afraid your Daddy is very sick.'

'What do you mean?'

'The doctor examined him and they did some tests. They found a tumour on his brain. I'm afraid he only has a few months to live,' said Mablean sadly.

Jake broke down and cried and Tina put her arms around him to comfort him.

'I want to see my Daddy,' said Jake.

'We'll take you to see him tomorrow,' said Mablean. Jake did not sleep much that night.

Next day, Lisa and Tina rolled him out to the car and maneuvered him into the front seat. They got into the back and Mablean drove to Princess Margaret Hospital.

They made their way through the hospital to Douglas's room. When Jake saw his father lying, there connected to life support machines, with tubes going in and out of him, tears started rolling down his cheeks. Jake sat at his father's bedside all day and refused to leave. He sat there in despair watching his father slowly deteriorate.

A month later Douglas died. In his will he left Jake all his earthly belongings. Since Jake had no other living relatives, Mablean decided to let him live with her, her twin daughters and granddaughter.

Mablean wanted to make Jake as comfortable as possible so she put the house that Jake and Douglas had lived in on rent. With the rent money she built another bedroom onto her house with a big walk in shower for Jake. The shower had a plastic bench so that they could sit Jake on it and shower him. Jake grieved for Douglas but he was happy in his new family.

The End

A ROUGH LIFE

By Michael Wells.

Roman was rolling down East Street in his chrome-plated wheelchair with a depressed look on his handsome face when a light blue Honda pulled alongside him and a man stuck his head out of the car window.

'Hi, Roman. What's happening?'

'Hey, Anderson,' replied Roman in a low voice.

'What happened to you? Why do you look so sad?'

'I'm depressed because I'm tired of Daddy's constant whining and complaining,' said Roman.

'Your Daddy loves you. He wouldn't do anything to hurt you,' said Anderson.

'I know that. But you can't imagine how irritating and annoying it is to have to listen to the same thing over and over. Daddy still talks about things that happened forty years ago and I'm tired of hearing about them.'

'Have you told him how you feel?'

'Yes, I have but he doesn't listen to me. I also asked a friend to talk to him but he won't listen to him either.'

'I can't say I know how you feel because I'm not in your position. But in my opinion, you should keep telling him how much he's upsetting you. He may not listen but at least he will know how you feel.' Anderson said.

'I'll keep trying but I doubt it will do any good.'

'Listen, I'm going to the Fish Fry tonight. Would you like to come with me? Maybe that will cheer you up.'

Roman hesitated and then he agreed. He appreciated his friend's kindness.

'I'll ask Patrina and Braquel to come with us. Let's say I'll pick you up at seven thirty.'

'I'll be ready.'

Anderson drove away and Roman rolled home. He found his father Owen, a grey-headed man, sitting on the porch.

'Well, the prodigal son has returned,' said Owen. 'The church is having a party tonight for the people whose birthdays are in June. Would you like to go?'

'No, I do not want to go,' said Roman.

'Why not? You'll enjoy yourself,' urged Owen.

'Why do you always do this? I tell you I don't want to do something and you always try to force me to do it,' said Roman bitterly.

'I'm only trying to make you comfortable.'

Roman rolled inside the messy house and into his bedroom where he changed his clothes. He rolled back outside just as Anderson pulled up. Roman maneuvered himself into the car while Anderson folded his chair and placed it in the trunk. They drove to a yellow and green house located in Chippingham.

Anderson blew the car horn and two beautiful young ladies stepped out and jumped into the car.

'Hi, Roman,' said the short bright skinned lady.

'Hi, Patrina. How's my little sweetie doing?' replied Roman.

'I'm fine.'

'Are you ready to have fun?' Roman enquired with a mischievous look.

'You'd better behave yourself,' said Patrina.

'I think that he wants to get frisky with you!' said Braquel.

'Patrina knows I have the hots for her,' said Roman.

When they reached the Fish Fry, everyone jumped out and Anderson removed the chair from the trunk and pushed it to the passenger door for Roman.

They went down to the Twin Brothers and sat on a bench. They ordered conch fritters and daiquiris.

'So Patrina, what are you doing later tonight?' asked Roman with a twinkle in his eye.

'I'm going to bed,' she replied.

'Do you want company?'

'No.'

'Come on, give your boy a break,' said Roman with a sly look.

'Drink another daiquiri and cool down,' said Patrina.

'I don't want another daiquiri, I want human contact.'

'What's happened to you tonight?' said Braquel. 'You seem troubled.'

'You all see me sitting here joking around and laughing but you don't know how I really feel,' said Roman.

'Come on, then. Tell us how you really feel,' said Patrina.

'There are times when I feel like running away and never coming back.'

'What's the problem?'

'My Daddy. He's getting more and more difficult. It's so frustrating and irritating to keep hearing the same thing over and over again. I have to be so careful when I'm doing anything around the house. If I make the slightest mistake, he goes ballistic.' As he spoke, Roman could not prevent the tears from rolling down his cheeks.

'It's very sad you have to live that way,' said Patrina gently.

'I think you should tell your Daddy exactly how you feel,' said Braquel. 'Make him listen so he knows how much he upsets you.

'I agree,' said Patrina.

Later that evening, the three friends dropped Roman home. He rolled in the front door and found Owen sitting in the living room watching wrestling on TV.

'I would like to talk to you,' said Roman.

'About what?'

'I'm tired of hearing you tell the same stories over and over. You think that everything I say is a joke. You never take me seriously and you don't listen to me,' said Roman. He took a deep breath, glad that he'd got it off his chest.

Owen turned off the TV and addressed his son.

'I do my best to try and keep you happy and to provide for you. And I notice that since you've gotten involved with these people you hang out with, you have changed.'

'I know you're doing your best and I really appreciate what you do, but you make it extremely hard for me to love you because you're such a perfectionist. There's absolutely nothing wrong with wanting things done right but you don't have to chase people and cuss them out just because they didn't do something precisely the way you want it done,' said Roman.

'I just want things done properly,' said Owen.

'I understand that but why do you always have to handle situations so angrily?'

'I'm sorry if I make you unhappy. In future I'll try and listen when you tell me things.'

'And another thing, stop forcing me to do things and go places that I don't want to. I have a mind of my own and if you ask me to go somewhere and I say no, please don't keep bugging me about it.'

'You always seem to like parties and the people would just love to see you.'

'I don't feel like going so stop asking me.'

'OK,' said Owen. 'I'll stop.'

Roman rolled into his room leaving Owen to think about their conversation. He hadn't realized that he was hurting his son so badly. He made an effort to stop doing the things that irritated and annoyed his son.

The End

PEGGY

By Michael Wells.

Peggy rolled into Super Value and pushed herself through the aisles in her wheelchair looking for the tuna fish. She found some but the cans were on the top shelf and she had to stretch up to reach them.

Some of the cans fell off the shelf and rolled about on the floor.

'Let me help you,' said a neatly dressed, handsome man. He picked up the cans and handed them to her.

'Thank you. Things would be so much easier if everything was accessible,' said Peggy.

'Some people don't think about persons with disabilities.'

'They certainly don't.'

'May I ask your name?' enquired the stranger.

'My name is Peggy Cunningham.'

'Very nice to meet you Ms. Cunningham. My name is Troy Darville.'

'Delighted to meet you, Mr. Darville.'

'You seem to be an extremely independent lady.'

'I am. I don't ask for help unless I really have to.'

'That's good. I know some people who don't do anything to help themselves but you are the complete opposite.'

'I refuse to let the disability I have stop me from living an active and productive life.'

'I admire that and I wish you success in everything you do.'

'Thank you for the compliment.' Peggy could not stop herself from blushing.

'Your boyfriend must be proud of you.'

'I don't have a boyfriend.'

'A beautiful lady like you doesn't have a boyfriend?'

Peggy gathered her things together and prepared to carry on with her shopping.

'You really know how to flatter a lady!'

'Can I call you sometime?'

'I don't know.'

'I'm working on a project and maybe you can help me with it?'

'What kind of project?'

'I want to open an exercise gym for persons with disabilities.'

Peggy looked at Troy with new interest.

'Really! That's a very good idea.'

'I came up with the plan when I was in Toronto. I visited a place called Variety Village where people with disabilities go to exercise and socialize,' said Troy.

'We need something like that in The Bahamas.'

'I agree and that's why I want to open a gym just for persons with disabilities.'

'I would be glad to help you. What would you like me to do?'

'Perhaps you can give me some advice on how to design the gym and how to make it accessible?'

'I would be delighted to help.'

'Would you like to come by my office so I can show you the plans so far?'

'Sure, I can.'

'How about one o'clock today? My office is located in the building opposite the old City Market on Rosetta Street,' said Troy.

'I know where that is. I'll be there at one o'clock sharp.'

Peggy finished her shopping and rolled out of the store. Troy came out behind her and watched as she manoeuvred herself into her van and drove off.

She drove home and entered her immaculately kept house. When she had put away the groceries, she rolled into the living room and switched on the computer. She checked her emails and signed into Facebook. She saw that her niece was on and hailed her.

'Hi Cassandra. How's everything with you?'

'Everything is fine. I just came home from the food store,' said Cassandra.

'Me, too!' said Peggy.

'I have something you might like,' said Cassandra. 'Two tickets for a concert. Would you like to come with me?'

'What date is the concert?'

'Next Saturday.'

'Sure, I would love to go.'

'It's at the National Theatre for the Performing Arts and it starts at seven thirty.'

'Would you like me to pick you up?' Peggy asked.

'Yes, that would be great.'

'I'll collect you at seven o'clock.'

Peggy rolled into her bedroom to freshen up then maneuvered into her van and drove to Troy's office.

She rolled her wheelchair easily through the wide doorway and spoke to the secretary. 'May I see Mr. Darville, please?'

'May I ask who is calling?'

'Ms. Cunningham,' said Peggy.

The secretary picked up the phone and informed Troy that Peggy was there to see him.

Peggy followed the secretary into his office.

'It's so nice to see you again,' said Troy, standing up from behind his desk to shake her hand.

‘Nice to see you again too,’ said Peggy.

‘I’m glad you could come.’

‘Your idea sounds good and I would like to learn more about creating an accessible gym.’

‘I’m delighted you’re so enthusiastic about it. I have the plans over here.’

Troy walked over to a filing cabinet and pulled open a drawer. He removed the plans and laid them on the desk.

Peggy spent a minute or two going over everything carefully.

‘This is very good,’ she said. ‘But how are you going to finance it?’

‘Don’t worry. I have the financial side of things straight,’ Troy assured her.

‘Congratulations. You seem to have everything well organized.’

‘So, you approve?’

‘Yes, I do and I wish you every success.’

‘Thank you and I hope you will stay associated with the project.’

‘I will assist you in any way I can.’

Troy seemed very happy with her reply.

‘Have you had lunch yet?’ he asked. ‘We could go to the Outback Steakhouse.’

‘That would be very nice.’

‘Can I ride with you?’

Troy held the door open and Peggy rolled outside. She got into the van while Troy climbed into the passenger seat.

When they arrived at the Outback Steakhouse, they were shown to their table and given a menu by the waitress.

When they had given their order, Troy turned to her and said warmly: ‘You really inspire me.’

‘Well, thank you,’ said Peggy shyly.

‘Have you ever thought about getting married?’

‘No, not really.’

‘I think you would make someone a wonderful wife.’

‘Are you serious?’

‘Yes, I’m very serious.’

‘You want to marry me?’

‘Yes, I do. You have many qualities that I admire and I’ve fallen in love with you.’ Troy replied as he kissed her.

‘I have to think about this.’

'OK. You take all the time you need. I'll wait for you to decide.'

They spent a pleasant hour together and then left the restaurant. Peggy dropped Troy at his office and drove home. She found Cassandra waiting by the house when she arrived.

'I didn't know you were coming,' said Peggy.

'I came to invite you to a party I'm having Friday night at my house,' said Cassandra.

'I'd love to come. What time is it?'

'The party starts at seven thirty.'

'Can I bring someone?'

'Sure, you can. Bring anyone you want.'

'I'd like you to meet my friend. He's so nice and sweet,' said Peggy, smiling.

'Does my Auntie have a boyfriend?'

'I guess you could say that.'

'I'm so happy for you.'

'I'm glad I met him and he makes me feel good.' She hesitated. 'But there's something about him that just doesn't sit right.'

'What do you mean?'

'I don't quite know what it is but there's something fishy about him.'

'If you feel that way then why don't you just tell him to get lost?'

'I think I may do that . . . after the party.'

'Good and don't let him sway you. If you need backup, you know who to call.'

'Thank you! You'll be the first person I call!'

After Cassandra left, Peggy picked up the cordless phone and called Troy.

'Would you like to come to a party with me at my niece's house on Friday?' she asked.

'I'd love to,' said Troy.

'I'll pick you up at seven.'

'I can't wait to see you,' said Troy.

When Friday came, Peggy dressed and drove her van to Troy's house. She blew the horn and he came out to join her. They drove to a white and green house located in Garden Hills. The house was full of people standing around talking. They made their way towards Cassandra.

'Hi Auntie,' she said. I'm happy you could make it.'

'This is my friend Troy. Troy, this is my niece Cassandra.'

'Nice to meet you,' said Troy.

'It's a pleasure to meet you, too,' replied Cassandra.

'I see that beauty runs in the family.'

'Well, thank you. You are a charmer.'

As they were speaking, a woman came to join them and pushed herself in front of Troy. He stepped back in shock.

'You told me you were going to Canada!' said the woman angrily.

Troy looked embarrassed and struggled to find his words.

'I finished my business in Canada and decided to come back to Nassau,' he said finally.

'Well why didn't you call me?'

'I forgot.'

'You forgot to call your wife?'

'Wife!' said Peggy. 'Troy, what's going on? Who is this woman?'

'Troy, tell this crippled woman who I am,' the woman said unpleasantly.

'This is my wife,' said Troy.

'Your wife! Troy please tell me it's not true?' said Peggy.

Troy was unable to look Peggy in the eyes.

Cassandra put her arm round her aunt and pointed Troy angrily towards the door.

'I think you'd better leave before I do something that will cause me to go to jail,' she said.

Troy left, followed by his wife who was still shouting at him.

Later it was learnt that Troy was married to three other women at the same time in different countries. Peggy couldn't believe that someone who had shown her so much kindness and care would do such a cruel, mean thing.

Troy was arrested and charged with bigamy. He was sentenced to three years in jail. Peggy never saw him again.

The End

A SCHOLARLY GENTLEMAN

By Michael Wells.

Ernest was sitting on the porch in his blue wheelchair enjoying the warm sunshine when he smelt a pungent odour coming from his neighbour's backyard. He rolled over to the fence and the odour got stronger.

He rolled to the front of the yard and found the smell there was not as strong.

'Do you smell an offensive odour?' he asked his neighbour, Ms. Beneby.

'Do you mean that stink coming from Mr. Archer's yard?' asked the grey-haired lady.

'Yes, I've being inhaling it all morning,' said Ernest.

'I can smell it, too. I don't know what it is,' said Ms. Beneby.

'Have you seen Mr. Archer today?'

'I haven't. He usually takes a walk in the morning but these past few mornings I haven't seen him.'

'I hope he's OK.'

'I'm sure he'll pop up,' said Ms. Beneby.

A brown Nissan pulled up and a tall man jumped out.

'Mr. Archer!' exclaimed Ms. Beneby. 'We were just talking about you.'

'Really! I hope you were saying good things about me.'

'We were wondering what had happened to you.'

'I was helping a friend fix her car,' said Mr. Archer.

'You're so kind. Always helping people,' said Ms. Beneby.

'I can't see someone in need and not assist them.'

Ernest had listened to this conversation.

'I think there's something dead in your backyard,' he said.

'Why do you say that?'

'There's an offensive smell coming from your yard.'

'That must be the rat my cat killed. I have to bury it. I'd better go and deal with it.'

Mr. Archer walked into his house and shortly afterwards a red Toyota pulled up. A glamorous lady jumped out and rushed up to Ernest and Ms Beneby.

'I just came from Sceiska and she's in a terrible state.'

'Calm down, Camille. What's happened?' said Ms. Beneby kindly.

'Sceiska's young daughter, Dana, has gone missing.'

'That's dreadful. How long has she been missing?'

'She's been gone since Thursday. Sceiska has reported her missing to the police.'

'Dana's a good girl. She doesn't go off by herself and she doesn't keep bad company,' said Ms. Beneby. 'And she gets good grades in school.'

'I pray they find her,' said Ernest.

'I should go to Sceiska,' said Ms. Beneby. 'to see if I can comfort her.'

'Would you like me to take you?' offered Camille.

'Thank you, I would.' The old lady turned to Ernest. 'I'll see you when I get back.'

While Ernest stayed on the porch watching the Archer property, Ms. Beneby and Camille drove to a white house located in Sea Breeze where their friend Sceiska lived.

Ms. Beneby rang the doorbell and hugged the slender woman who opened it. 'How are you doing?' she asked.

'I'm trying to make it. These past few days have been really rough,' said Sceiska.

'I can only imagine what you're going through.'

'I haven't been able to sleep since Dana has been gone. I don't know where my baby is.'

'What did the police say?'

'They're looking for her. And other people are, too.'

'They'll find her. You just keep praying.'

'I do that every day and I know that God will answer my prayers.'

'Yes, He will. Is there anything I can do for you?' asked Camille.

'No thanks. I just want my Dana back.' Tears rolled down Sceiska's chocolate brown cheeks.

'Everything will be all right.' Ms. Beneby put her arms around Sceiska to comfort her.

'I miss my little girl so much.'

Later that day Camille dropped Ms. Beneby home and left to attend a meeting. Ms. Beneby was walking to her front door when Ernest hailed her.

'Hello, Ms. Beneby.'

'Hi Ernest. Whatcha saying?'

'I think Mr. Archer is up to something,' said Ernest.

'Why do you say that?'

'While I was outside, I saw Mr. Archer moving a huge freezer into his house.'

'What's so strange about that?'

'What's he doing with a freezer that size? What's he storing?'

'I don't know. Maybe he has some fish?'

'Maybe. But that freezer would sure hold a lot fish. He lives by himself. What's he going to do with all that fish?'

'I really don't know,' said Ms. Beneby.

'It just seems strange.'

'If you really want to know. Why don't you ask him?'

Ernest bid her goodnight, rolled into his house and lay down in the bedroom. He had drifted off to sleep when he was suddenly awakened by a bright light beaming in through the window. He manoeuvred into his chair and rolled over to the window.

What he saw amazed him. Mr. Archer was digging a deep, wide hole in his backyard. He carried big boxes from the house and heaved them into the hole. Ernest couldn't wait to find out what was in them. When Mr. Archer walked back into the house, Ernest rolled over silently onto the property and looked in one of the boxes. He was shocked to discover human body parts. As fast as he could, he rolled to the police station and reported what he had found.

The police drove back with Ernest and found Mr. Archer refilling the hole with dirt. The police opened the boxes and were horrified to see the body parts inside.

They handcuffed Archer and placed him into the patrol car. He was taken to the interrogation room at the police station.

'Why were you burying body parts in your backyard?' asked Officer Bell.

'I was finished with them and I was getting rid of the parts I didn't want,' said Archer.

'What on earth do you mean? Finished with them?'

'I was conducting an experiment, transplanting the brain of one person into another person.'

Officer Bell shook his head. He had never heard anything like it.

'How did you come up with that crazy idea?'

'I just thought it would be fun.'

The police realised they were dealing with a psychopath.

'Where did you get the bodies to work on?'

'I chose my subjects randomly.'

'How many people did you used in your . . . experiment?'

'About twenty people.'

'So, there are twenty people buried in your backyard?'

'Yes, that's right.' Archer spoke with a sense of pride.

'You don't have any remorse for what you did?'

'Nope. I did it all for science.' He leaned back in his chair and laughed.

Archer appeared in court next day and was charged with murder. He was found guilty and sentenced to hang. He was hanged on 22nd June 2015.

When the police dug up the bodies that Archer had buried, they found Dana's body.

The End

PHOTOS

Michael with his father, Roderick Wells

Michael with Shirley Francis (mother), Cheryl Wells (sister)
and Van Wells (nephew) in the Anglican Diocesan Car Park, Nassau,
where he sells his books

Candace Brown, Illustrator of this book

Eric Minns, who illustrated Books 1-7.

Michael with Lesley Spencer, editor, and Book 7
which was published in 2017

Made in the USA
Columbia, SC
03 April 2019